PAT LOWE & JI

Yinti's
desert dog

Magabala
Books

First published 1997
New edition 2019, reprinted 2019 x2, 2021 x2
Magabala Books Aboriginal Corporation
1 Bagot Street, Broome, Western Australia
Website: www.magabala.com
Email: sales@magabala.com

Magabala Books receives financial assistance from the
Commonwealth Government through the Australia Council,
its arts advisory body. The State of Western Australia has
made an investment in this project through the Department of
Local Government, Sport and Cultural Industries. Magabala
Books would like to acknowledge the support of the Shire of
Broome, Western Australia.

Design Jo Hunt
Printed and bound by Griffin Press, South Australia

Print   978-1-925936-90-2
ePDF   978-1-925936-91-9
ePUB   978-1-925936-92-6

 A catalogue record for this
book is available from the
National Library of Australia

 Department of
**Local Government, Sport
and Cultural Industries**
  Australian Government

About the series

All the books in the Yinti series are based on true incidents told to me by Jimmy Pike from his own life. I have fictionalised and expanded the stories, adding details from my own imagination and experience of the country in which they take place. Taken together, they show Yinti's progress from his desert boyhood to life as a competent station worker.

Desert Dog, the second book in the series, begins from the point of view of wild dingoes, and only later do human beings enter the story. Yinti and his tame dingo, Spinifex, travel north and have their first experience of cattle stations. While Yinti soon adapts to life there, Spinifex is spooked by the noise and chaos, and goes missing.

Pat Lowe

Contents

Prologue

It was a cool desert morning. The sky was clear from horizon to horizon and a keen, dry wind was blowing from the east. Two dingo pups were playing in the sandhills near their den, while their mother was away hunting for food. They chased and wrestled and bit one another, and rolled over and over in the sand. Danger was far from their young minds.

A bird flew up into a nearby tree, and called out shrilly:

"Peoplepeople! Peoplepeople!"

The urgency of the bird's call brought the pups to a sudden standstill. They listened, their small bodies taut, their nostrils twitching. Again the bird called its warning:

"Peoplepeople! Peoplepeople!"

A scent of danger reached them on the wind. Another moment and they felt a vibration through the ground. One of the pups turned and raced to the den; his fluffy hindquarters disappeared inside. The second pup hesitated just a moment too long. The scent of human being and the vibrating footfall were almost upon her. She skittered across the sand and burrowed into the closest clump of spinifex. The grass pierced her skin and pricked her nose, but she barely noticed, so great was her terror. She cowered there and lay as still as she could.

The footsteps paused, then started again, coming closer and closer to the pup's hiding place, until the human being stood huge above her. The pup shut her eyes, breathing suspended. Suddenly, the figure stooped, a hand descended through the grass, and the pup felt herself being seized by the scruff of the neck and lifted into the air. She cringed, waiting for death.

Instead, she found herself squeezed against the massive human body. The people-scent filled her nostrils and instinctively she ducked her head, forcing it down between the imprisoning limb and the woman's breast.

The woman's body was cool and firm. The pup, almost dead with fear, was aware of movement, but little else. She was jogged from side to side as the woman walked. The regular movement, the soft breast, lulled the pup and, after a while, when still no harm had come to her, her terror began to lessen.

At length, the woman stopped walking and the pup heard the sounds of other human beings. She shrank down further between limb and body, but now different hands seized her. She was carried away from the woman and raised above another head. Dark eyes gazed at her, impossibly close, and a boy laughed. She was too frightened to struggle and hung passively, waiting for whatever might come. But still she did not die.

The young hands that now held her were rougher than those of the woman and the boy's voice loud in her ear. She felt a morsel of meat pushed against her nose, but the pup had no interest in food and turned away her head.

As the day went on and no one harmed her, the pup began to feel less afraid. She became aware of thirst and awkwardly lapped up water the woman offered in her cupped palm. She missed the comfort of her mother's flanks, of her familiar scent, her milk, yet already she was getting used to human beings.

That night the pup slept curled in the crook of the woman's arm.

Chapter one

The female dingo lay crouched near the crest of a sandhill, behind a screen of wattle bushes. Beside her, subdued by their mother's urgent nudging, sat her two young pups. On the flat below them, unaware that their every movement was being watched, a family of human beings was going about its business.

Though the dingo was silent, her behaviour spoke to her pups. They read the fear that had sent the hackles rising on her back when she had first caught the scent of the human beings. They understood the cautious way she had slunk along the sandhill to look down on the camp.

The human beings had made fire and they were cooking game. The watching dingoes could smell the singeing meat and they drooled.

But there was danger in lingering near a human camp and in a little while the mother dingo led her pups silently away, leaving the family of human beings to finish their meal. The following morning, not long after the sun came up, the dingo mother went back alone to the sandhill above the camp of the human beings. Before she set off, she instructed her pups to stay behind. With her muzzle, she pushed them back into their den in the sand, and when they tried to follow her, she growled a warning. They understood and obeyed.

The dingo made her way to the camp, trotting easily through the spinifex in the cool of the early morning. She kept her head low. Human beings were unpredictable. One of those she had seen the day before might come walking this way. As she climbed the sandhill above the camp, she scented the air. Were they still around or had they gone?

From behind the wattle bushes, she looked down over the camping place below. Nothing moved. A wisp of smoke rising from the dying fire was the only sign of life. Still the dog stayed where she was, alert and watching.

When she was sure no one was around the camp, the dingo sloped down the side of the sandhill to the flat. Moving quickly, alert for any sound, she headed towards the remains of the cooking fire. She sniffed all around the fireplace and amongst the ashes. She found nothing but a few scraps of charred skin, which she swallowed in an instant. Further from the fire, she smelt something more appetising and picked up a small bone with shreds of meat still attached. She carried the bone into the shelter of a tussock of long grass and ate it quickly, crunching it into a few small pieces before gulping them down. Back she went for another quick search of the camp. She found a second bone, which she ate where she stood, all the time alert and watchful in case any of the human beings should return.

After so many years of living near to human beings, she had learnt their habits. She knew the signs of an abandoned camp — the dead fireplace, the absence of belongings. When people went away for a long time, or for good, they took everything with them. When they left objects of wood and stone behind, smelling strongly of their touch, or a fire banked up and covered, but still alive inside, she knew they would come back. These people had left behind a number of articles — a large wooden vessel, still with a trace of water in the bottom, which the dingo now licked up quickly; some narrow lengths of wood, cut from tall saplings and sharpened at one end, which the males often carried with them and used as weapons to kill animals like herself. And there were stone tools — a big, flat rock with hollows worn in its surface and a smaller rock, just the right size to be held in a human hand. The dingo didn't know that these tools were used by the female human beings for grinding grass and wattle seeds when they were preparing food. She knew them only as signs that the people had not gone for good.

When she had explored all around the camp and picked up every scrap of bone and discarded skin, the dingo started back to her pups.

Meanwhile, the two young pups had not been lying down quietly, waiting for their mother to come back to them with food. They stayed in the den for a while, sleeping. Then they woke up and wanted to play. One, and then the other, came to the entrance of their hole in the sand and peeped out. All was quiet. Only a few harmless little birds were feeding on the flowers of the honey trees growing nearby. Then a small lizard darted by in front of them. With no further thought of caution, the two pups were out of their hole and after the lizard. It disappeared into a tuft of grass. One pup jumped and landed stiffly in the grass on all four paws, sure she had

trapped the lizard. The other snuffled about, forcing his nose into the tussock of spiny grass. By the time they realised the lizard had tricked them, it was already well away.

The two pups started a mock fight, biting one another's ears and rolling over and over in the soft sand. By now they had completely forgotten their mother's warnings about danger, and her instructions to stay inside their den while she was away. One of the pups wandered off to sniff around in a patch of grass. Suddenly, a dark shadow crossed the ground in front of her. An eaglehawk! Without stopping to look up, the pup lowered her head and fled at full speed towards the lair. Her twin, infected with his sister's panic, ran behind her. As he raced homewards, he too glimpsed the eaglehawk's threatening shadow.

Fortunately for the two pups, they hadn't strayed far and were safely back inside their burrow before the eaglehawk could swoop on them. They lay huddled together shivering, not even daring to look out and see whether the eaglehawk was waiting in a tree nearby or had flown away.

Just as their mother had taught the pups to fear human beings, so she had taught them to beware of the eaglehawk. The great bird was powerful enough to carry off an animal as big as a wallaby; an unwary dingo pup would be easy prey.

When the dingo mother at last came back from foraging, she could tell at once that her pups hadn't stayed in hiding. She smelt their fresh tracks outside the burrow where they had played. They were not in sight now, but neither was there any sign of danger. All the same, she hurried to her den. She was relieved to find her pups safe, though a little subdued. They greeted her with whimpers of pleasure and she nuzzled them. Then she brought up from her own stomach the chewed bones and meat scraps she had swallowed at the people's camp. Her pups ate the warm, soft mixture hungrily.

As she fed them, the female dingo thought uneasily about her mate. He had left camp the previous afternoon. He had headed north to hunt at a waterhole some way off. He should have been home by now.

Chapter two

The male dingo was an older dog with long experience in the life of the desert and the ways of its inhabitants. For much of the hotter part of the year, he and his mate lived independent lives, hunting their own game, staying apart for days at a time, then meeting up and travelling together for a while before separating again. Early in the cooler time, when the urge to mate was upon them, they lived closely as a pair once more. They dug a deep den in the sand and slept there together. While the female dingo was heavy with pup, and afterwards, when she had given birth and was feeding the young with her milk, her old mate went out alone each day and brought back meat for her.

The two pups she had carried this year were not her first. The dingo mates had reared litters of two and three pups in previous seasons. Those young dogs had lived in the sandhills near their parents during much of their first year of life. They had learned how to hunt and where to look for water, gradually becoming more capable of providing for themselves. Once they were fully independent, it was time for them to move away and find mates of their own.

The old male dingo was a skilled hunter and provided well for his family while the pups were very young. He regularly brought game to his mate: freshly caught goannas, birds and sometimes even cats. It took a lot of effort and skill to hunt down a cat. He could follow a cat for a long way and just when he was about to seize it, the cunning animal would spurt forward and rapidly

climb a tree trunk. Then the dingo would hide and wait patiently in the grass until the cat believed he had gone or was driven down from the tree by hunger. This was the dingo's chance to take the cat by surprise. He would wait until the cat was a safe distance from the tree, then rush out and leap on it before it had a chance to get away. Scars on his muzzle and ears bore witness to the fight that always followed.

He set off hunting at around dusk, and usually came home at dawn. If the night's catch had been poor, he might stay out longer, returning later in the morning. He never failed to bring back something for his family to eat. He would vomit onto the ground the lizards he had swallowed whole, for his mate and her pups.

Now that the pups were getting old enough to be left alone for short spells and even to accompany their mother on some of her forays nearby, she too had started hunting again. But she dared not leave her pups for long and didn't like to venture too far from their camp. Mother and young still depended in part on the meat the old male dog brought home for them.

But this day, the male dog did not come.

The female dingo waited for him all the morning and into the afternoon. She had almost weaned her pups and the food she had brought back for them in the morning was not enough to keep them satisfied for long. By late in the day, the pups were nudging their mother again for meat, but she had none to give them.

By nightfall the pups' hunger and her own uneasiness drove her to action. After letting the pups drink what they could draw from her teats, she left them sleeping sprawled on top of one another in the den. Then she set off in the same direction her mate had taken the day before.

She followed his tracks for a long way. She found the place where her mate had run after and caught a goanna; she came upon the remains of a bush turkey, killed earlier in the day by an eaglehawk, and knew that the male dingo had stopped to feed from the carcass. She sniffed at the clump of grass where he had squirted urine afterwards.

Suddenly, the hackles rose between her shoulders and along her back as another, different scent stimulated her nostrils. It was the scent of a female human being. And the human scent was mingled with that of the male dingo. The woman had been following him.

They were not like dingoes, these upright creatures. Sometimes they behaved as if they had no sense of smell at all. The female dingo knew that an animal could be

upwind of a human being, not far away, yet the human would show no sign of having sensed its presence. At other times, as now, they had an uncanny ability to follow tracks, upwind or down, without smelling them.

Filled with dread, the dingo followed the double scent — that of her mate overlain with the scent of the human being — until she came to the place where the two had met. There was a shallow depression in the sand where the male dingo had lain down to rest and, much too close, the tracks of the human being.

In agitation, the female dingo ran about with her muzzle close to the ground. Her sense of smell told her all she needed to know. Her mate's scent still lingered in the hollow where he had slept, and in the tracks he had made as, in sudden agony, he had sprung up and started to run, blood spurting from his mouth. She smelt the place where the old dog had staggered and fallen, struggled to get up and fallen back, his limbs working uselessly until his heart gave out and he lay still. And there was a dark stain that had soaked into the sand where she could smell the old dog's lifeblood.

She had not seen the woman brace her foot against the dingo's side to pull out the spear. She had not seen her bend down and heave the dingo's lifeless body onto her back and arrange it across her shoulders. But the female dingo could smell the blood that had dripped down the woman's flanks as she walked.

The dingo sat back on her haunches, raised her head and pointed her muzzle towards the sky. The wind carried her long-drawn-out cry far across the sandhills.

Chapter three

After losing her companion, the female dingo grieved and, for a time, she kept well away from the human beings' camp. But now she alone must meet the urgent demands of her pups and soon she started to go back to the camp to scavenge for leftover pieces of food. Although she was able to hunt enough game to support herself and her pups, she was glad of the morsels of cooked meat the humans left behind. She might spend a great deal of time and energy hunting a live animal and, while doing so, would have to leave the pups unprotected, but in the camp she sometimes picked up substantial bones at the cost of very little effort. So long as she only went to the camp after the human beings had left, or at night, as she sometimes did, while they slept, she was not in any great danger and her pups stayed safely hidden in their den.

But the female dingo did not reckon on the depth of cunning of human beings.

The people were well aware that a dingo was visiting their camp while they were away during the day. Each afternoon when they came back from hunting, they looked for her tracks and saw where she had prowled around looking for food. They found the places where she had picked up a morsel of bone or of skin. Some of the scraps she found, they had deliberately left for her.

One afternoon two boys followed the tracks from the camp, up over the sandhill, past the wattles where the female dingo had once hidden with her pups, and down the far side. They saw that the tracks came and went always in the same direction.

'That dingo must have pups,' the elder boy told his mother. He spoke the language of the desert people. 'She always goes north from here.'

'Yes, it's the right time,' said his mother. 'The honey trees are in flower. The pups should be a good size by now.'

'I'll look for them tomorrow,' said the elder boy, whose name was Yinti.

'I'll come with you,' said his little brother Kana.

'No,' said the woman. 'I'll go. If the dingo mother finds you stealing her pups, she'll attack you and maul you. She might even kill you.'

Next morning, Yinti's mother set off to follow the tracks of the female dingo. Just as her son had said, they headed north, along a well-used trail. The coldest part of the year was now over, but a brisk wind was blowing from the east and the morning air was chilly.

The woman walked quickly. She carried a hunting stick and a short spear made by her husband from the trunk of a young turtujarti, a desert nut tree. As she went, she remembered the big male dingo she had tracked and speared not long ago.

The woman crossed two more sandhills and the flat country in between before she found what she was looking for. In amongst the dingo's tracks were lots of smaller ones. The woman studied them for a moment and made out two small sets. They ran all over the sand in between the tufts of grass, where the two pups had rolled and played.

For an experienced hunter like this woman, it was now a simple matter to read from the tracks which way the pups had run to hide. The most recent tracks led to a clump of grass, from which none reappeared. Bending down, the woman reached into the grass and lifted out a cowering pup. It was female. She tucked it under her arm, holding it firmly against her chest with her hand, and started to look for the second pup. She soon found the low slit that was the opening of the lair in amongst the clumps of long grass. Still holding the captured pup, she knelt and pushed the grass aside until she could look into the lair. It was deep. She knew the other pup was in there, but she couldn't see it or reach it.

The woman hesitated. She could dig the pup out of the den, but she had no digging stick with her, and to break off a tree branch and then use it to dig with one

hand while she held the female pup in the other, would be difficult. Also, the mother dingo was very likely to come back. A female dingo defending its young was a vicious animal and the woman was not keen to face one now. She decided to be satisfied with the one pup. She or someone else could come back another time for the second. It would be all the better to eat when it was older and fatter. Meanwhile, she had other plans for the little dingo in her arms. She carried it back to her camp.

The woman's sons were delighted.

'Can we keep her, Mother?' begged Yinti. He was growing up now and learning to hunt, but he still had a soft spot for young animals. When he was smaller, if his mother or someone else killed a female kangaroo or possum with young in its pouch, they sometimes gave the baby to Yinti to play with. Once cooking time came, however much he begged to keep the little animal, his mother's answer was always the same.

'What would you feed it on?' she would say. 'You've got no milk.'

Then she would take the baby animal from her son's grasp and quickly kill it, then set it beside its mother in the fire.

Dingo pups were different. Though people usually

ate them, like other animals they caught, they sometimes spared the life of a pup. They kept it as a companion and trained it to hunt. As long as the pup was old enough to survive without its mother's milk, it could be fed on soft meat while it was small and grow up safely amongst human beings.

'Yes, I'll keep this one,' said the boys' mother. 'I'll grow her up and she can learn to hunt for us. She'll be my second daughter.'

The little pup was still terrified, too frightened even to struggle. She huddled passively in the woman's arms. Now Yinti took her and she cowered from his touch.

'I'll give her some meat,' he told his mother, and went to pull a few scraps from part of a wallaby carcass left hanging in a tree. He chewed the meat until it was soft, then spat it into his hand and offered it to the pup. She didn't respond. The boy pushed the meat against her mouth, trying to force her to take it, but she pulled away.

'She's still too frightened,' he said. 'I'll give her something later.'

For the rest of the day, he carried the pup around in his arms. If he put her on the ground, she immediately made a scramble for the nearest clump of spinifex, to hide. He could have left her there, knowing that at her young age she wouldn't go far, but he wanted her to get used to being with people.

By nightfall the little dingo had lapped some water from the woman's cupped hand and, when the boy again offered her meat from his own mouth, she swallowed it hungrily and looked for more.

That night she slept next to the woman, and by the following morning, she was ready to run about and play.

Chapter four

From that time on, the little dingo learnt to live with human beings. Though she had taken her first food from the hands of the boy, it was to the woman, whose name was Mala, that the pup attached herself. It was Mala who took the scent from her own armpits onto her hands and rubbed it on the dingo's nose to ensure her loyalty. Mala looked after her, fed her and took her everywhere she went. When the pup got tired of running along behind, Mala carried her. On cold nights, she slept close to Mala for warmth.

'This pup-daughter of mine is the colour of dry grass,' said Mala one day. 'I'll call her Spinifex.'

Like all dingoes, Spinifex was fiercely independent. As a pup, she was playful and self-willed. After sleeping for most of the day, she came to life in the cool of the afternoon. She raced around the camp, biting people and other dogs, wreaking havoc until someone gave her food. Every morning at first light, she practised hunting and chased tiny lizards into the tufts of sharp grass. She sprang into the air, all four feet off the ground, and landed, if she was lucky, with her front paws on top of a trapped lizard. More often, all she trapped was a tuft of grass.

Around the middle of the day, when the human beings stopped to rest and to cook the morning's catch, Spinifex would find a hiding place in deep grass, curl up small and go to sleep. When the meat was cooked and the people were eating, Mala would call out to Spinifex to come and get the scraps.

'Daughter!' she would call, and there would be no reply.

'Daughter!' she'd call again. Then, a sleepy young voice from somewhere in the scrub nearby would give a brief howl of acknowledgment. A few moments later, when she had shaken off the residue of sleep, the young dingo would appear at the fireside, ready to pick up the meat Mala had saved for her.

As Spinifex got older, she went hunting with Mala. At first she treated the hunt as play and wasted her energy chasing anything that caught her eye, bringing back lizards too small to eat. But Mala rubbed the blood of a goanna and the fluid from the gall bladder of a cat onto her nose and soon the young dog was learning to catch bigger game herself. She could pick up the scent of an animal and follow its track. She learnt how to dig a goanna out of its hole, to seize it between her jaws and to kill it with a quick, neck-snapping shake of her head.

Sometimes Spinifex got onto the trail of a cat. She ran ahead, much faster than Mala, and followed the trail back and forth as the cat tried to dodge away, gradually wearing it down. Cunning as the cat was, it could not shake off the dog. It got weaker and eventually could run no further. It might try, hopelessly, to hide in a patch of thick tussocks of sharp-pointed grass where Spinifex had no trouble sniffing it out. Then the cat would put up a last, desperate fight, teeth bared, ears flattened against its head, spitting and clawing. If Spinifex attacked it head on, it would sink its teeth into the skin of her face and rip her ears. She learnt to dart in and seize a cat by the back of its neck so that it was unable to scratch and bite her. With her jaws clamped around its neck and throat, she'd crush the life from it. But not all cats let themselves be killed so easily. A determined cat might keep up the fight until Mala, following the tracks at a run, arrived with her hunting stick.

'Leave it, now!' she would tell the dog and, with a couple of strong blows, she'd put an end to the cat's brave struggle.

Other times, a fleeing cat would escape the dog by running up the trunk of a desert tree and settle, panting, in amongst the upper branches. Spinifex, after flinging herself up at the tree in an effort to follow the cat, stood guard below. When Mala arrived, she aimed her hunting stick, threw it hard upwards through the branches and knocked the cat to the ground. It might be stunned or, not seriously injured, make a break for freedom. Either way, Spinifex was there to seize it. Though she often got scratched and bitten, Spinifex never gave up a chase.

Whenever she killed an animal by herself, Spinifex carried it to Mala.

'That's right!' Mala would tell her, approvingly. 'You're a good hunter!'

Then the woman took the game back to camp and cooked it in the fire while Spinifex watched. When the time came to distribute the cooked meat, Mala always gave some to Spinifex. The dog liked to eat meat that had been cooked in the fire. Besides her own portion,

Spinifex received the bones left by Mala and her children.

But Spinifex did more than help Mala catch game when they went hunting together. Sometimes, in the early, early mornings before the sun sent up the first rays of light, she went off hunting on her own. She trotted out from the camp and sniffed around until she came upon the scent of a fresh set of tracks.

Most desert animals move around at night, or in the very early hours of the morning before the heat of the day, and Spinifex knew that those were the best times to go hunting. She tracked her prey by its scent and then chased and caught it or dug it out of its hole and carried it back to camp to be cooked by Mala on the early morning fire.

Some mornings Spinifex might catch several animals, usually lizards of one sort or another. She would pick up two or even three goannas together by their heads and carry them back, their tails dragging on the ground. As she got close, she would call out: 'Mm! Mm! Mm! Mm!' If she'd had a really good morning's hunting and caught more animals than she could carry, Spinifex would bury some of them in the sand so that birds of prey couldn't spot them from the sky and steal them. Then she'd go back to camp, carrying perhaps a single goanna.

When Spinifex arrived at camp in the morning, Mala looked at her face. If there was sand or dirt sticking to her muzzle, Mala knew the dog had buried something.

'Ah, you've left some more meat for us, have you?' the woman would say. When she was ready, Mala would get up and follow Spinifex's tracks back to the places where the animals were buried and dig them out. In this way Spinifex saved Mala a lot of work and she soon became well known amongst the sandhill people as a fine hunting dog.

Chapter five

As Spinifex grew up, she learnt the habits of the human beings with whom she lived. They, like other beings of the desert, were always on the move. The rhythms of their lives were guided by the rhythms of the seasons and by their need for precious, widely dispersed sources of water and supplies of food.

Yinti and Kana were not Mala's only children. The eldest was her daughter Lilil, who had already left her parents to live with her husband. While Spinifex was growing up in the desert, Lilil was living far away on a cattle station to the north, where her husband worked for the kartiya — the white people. It was there she had her own first child.

Spinifex only knew Mala's two young sons. She

treated them like her own, helping to feed them with the meat she brought to their mother.

In her second year, after the end of the rainy time, when the weather was dry and starting to cool down, Spinifex found a mate. He was a dog that lived with one of Mala's nieces, who at that time was camping nearby with her family. After the waxing and waning of two moons, Spinifex gave birth to her first litter of pups. By then, her mate and his human family had moved on to another waterhole. But, unlike her own mother, Spinifex had no need of her mate's help to rear her young, for Mala and her children made sure the dogs were all safe and well fed.

Over the years that followed, Spinifex gave birth to several more litters of pups. She was a good mother; she guarded her pups fiercely while they were small, and shared with them the game she hunted. When the pups had grown strong enough to leave their mother's care, Mala gave them away to relations who had asked for them. Everyone who visited Mala, or travelled with her family and got to know Spinifex the hunting dog, wanted to have one of her pups, hoping it would inherit its mother's ability.

With her family of human beings, Spinifex travelled

around the waterholes that belonged to their country. In the course of each year they visited many of them and Spinifex eventually got to know them all. At each new camp, she went hunting for game.

Mala and her boys sometimes travelled alone. At other times, they met up with relations and moved around for a while in a larger group. They would stop near a waterhole and, if there was plenty of food to be gathered and game to be caught, they settled there for a time. Then, when food became scarce, they would move on to a place of greater abundance. Spinifex got used to meeting different people and, in time, she came to recognise most of Mala's relations.

Some waterholes, called jila, came from underground springs and were reliable, whatever the season. Others, such as jiwari, shallow rockholes, held water only when rain had fallen recently. Still others, known as jumu, were variable. During periods of drought, they would dry up completely but, following a good season of rain, they might hold water for several months. These realities of desert life directed the movements of the people.

In the hot-weather time at the end of the long dry season, when no rain had fallen for many months, all the temporary waterholes had run dry and hunting was more and more difficult, Mala and her family made their way back to Japingka, the biggest jila in their country. Here they were joined by many of their relations, all waiting for the rains to break. There were so many people living at the same place in that season that the game was soon hunted out. Spinifex had to travel a long way to find goannas and other animals. The human beings ate less meat but more of their vegetable foods, especially the nuts they collected from underneath the shady turtujarti trees. But Spinifex wasn't interested in eating vegetables and nuts. She wanted meat.

Once the rain started to fall, everyone moved out from Japingka. People broke up again into small family groups and went to camp at different waterholes as they filled up again.

One day, a small band of people arrived at Mala's camp. They were different from anyone Spinifex had seen before. They came from the north and, two days before they arrived, everyone in camp knew they were on their way. The smoke from their fires drifted over the sandhills on the morning air. Spinifex saw and smelt it too and looked uneasily at Mala. But there was excitement, not fear, in Mala's manner. When the travellers finally approached the camp, the people waiting there hurried forward to greet them and everyone started to cry. Spinifex backed away, her tail between her legs, and hid behind a clump of grass.

The newcomers carried with them strange scents of unfamiliar places. They even looked different from the people Spinifex knew. Their bodies were covered with garments of cloth, and they carried with them hard metal tools such as Spinifex had never seen. It was late in the day before she ventured out of hiding and tiptoed forward cautiously to sniff the strangers one by one.

One of these strange people was Mala's daughter, Lilil. She came with her husband, Kaj, and her own little girl, to visit her family in the desert. The other people in the group were more distantly related and, in a day or two, they moved on to find their own close families. Lilil's family stayed.

After a time, the visitors shed their clothes and took on the normal smell of their surroundings and, at last, seemed just like everyone else. But a year passed by and then they left again and travelled north, the way they had come. Spinifex didn't see them again for several years.

The next time Lilil and her family came to the sandhills, Spinifex was a dog in her middle years of life. She no longer raced around, playing and teasing people and biting them, as she had in her younger days. She was content to spend more time lying quietly in the shade,

keeping a watchful eye on the world around her. She had lost none of her hunting skill. Indeed, this had only improved as she got older and more experienced. All of Mala's relations knew Spinifex the hunting dog, and many would have liked to take her away with them, but Mala was never willing to part with her.

'She's my second daughter,' she'd say.

Chapter six

When the two families had been living together again in the sandhill country for about a year, Lilil gave birth to her second child, another little girl. Spinifex, who no longer had pups of her own, took great interest in the infant and sat watching over her whenever Lilil left her in a coolamon or on the sand, while she was busy collecting and cooking food. At such times, Spinifex would allow no one else near the child, nor did she leave her side until Lilil returned. The young woman grew fond of her mother's dog and she was glad to eat the game Spinifex still brought back to camp in the early mornings.

'She's the best hunting dog,' said Lilil to her mother. 'I'd like to have a dog of my own like that.'

Some months later, when the little girl was just starting

to crawl around, all the people set off to travel north into new territory. On the way, Mala's family was joined by a group of relations they hadn't seen for a very long time. Amongst them was Yinti's cousin and age-mate, Wara. The two boys walked and played and hunted together. Little Kana got left behind with his mother and only had his niece to play with.

Spinifex went along with all the people. She didn't know that some of them were planning to push right on into cattle station country. But she liked to be on the move and at each new waterhole she sniffed around the grass and trees until she had made herself familiar with the new scents. Then she set off to see what game the country had to offer. The travellers met no other human beings; only animals seemed to live in these new regions. Spinifex was as excited as a puppy to find herself in a land of such abundance.

At length, the party reached a waterhole, a jumu called Kajamuka, and camped there for one night. The next morning Spinifex sensed that some of the people were making preparations to leave. Lilil and her family were going back to the station.

'Can I go too?' Yinti asked his mother. She hesitated and Yinti pressed her.

'I want to go with Wara to visit the station. We want to see cattle. My sister can look after us. We'll come back next year.'

'Is Wara going?' asked his mother.

'Yes,' said Yinti. 'His mother says he can go if I go.'

'They'll be all right,' put in Lilil. 'I'll keep an eye on them.'

'All right, you two can go,' said Mala.

'And me?' asked little Kana hopefully.

'You're too young,' Yinti told him. 'You can come next time.'

For the first stage of the day's journey, Mala and Wara's parents walked along with the travellers to give them a start. They took their time, following tracks and catching game as they went. Around midday, everyone stopped to eat.

After a rest, when the sun was casting longer shadows, the travellers were ready to set off. Yinti and Wara stood up with the others.

Last words were said. Lilil spoke to her mother and Spinifex heard her own name and saw people looking at her. She pricked up her ears. As the little family group moved off, Lilil and Yinti called to Spinifex and the dog realised they wanted her to go with them. She looked at

Mala inquiringly, uncertain what to do, but Mala nodded her head.

'Go on,' she told her. 'You go with my daughter and son. Hunt for them — bring them plenty of game!' Though she had no idea how far from her country these people were planning to take her, Spinifex trotted along behind.

Soon Mala and the other people who stayed behind at Kajamuka waterhole were out of sight and out of smelling distance to Spinifex.

Chapter seven

The little group travelled always north. They seemed to be in a hurry to get somewhere. Instead of staying for several days at each waterhole as they did in their own country, they camped only for a single night, then moved on again the next day. Lilil carried a wooden coolamon of water on her head to last until they reached the next camp.

When the party left Kajamuka, rain had just started falling. This meant there should be water in the jumu soaks on which they would depend for most of the journey. But on the third day, they reached a waterhole where no rain had fallen. By now only a little water remained in the bottom of the coolamon.

It was a hot day and Spinifex was thirsty. Her feet were

sore from running on the burning sand and she lay down in the shade, panting. She watched Kaj bend down and dig in the ground with his hand. He picked up a handful of soil and tossed it lightly a few times. The breeze caught some of the soil each time it was tossed, until there was none left to fall back in his palm.

'Dry like dust,' he remarked. 'The rain wasn't as widespread as we thought.'

'The next living waterhole is many sandhills away,' said Lilil. 'It's too hot to keep going today — we'd perish of thirst. We'll have to stay here till it gets cooler.'

Kaj just grunted.

There was not enough water in the coolamon for everyone to have a drink. Lilil gave some to her daughters first because they were small. Then she tore up a hank of long dry grass, bent it in half to make it stiff, soaked the folded end in the water and handed it to Yinti.

'Just enough to wet your mouth,' she said.

Yinti sucked the moisture from the grass, then handed the grass to Wara, who dipped it into the shallow water and sucked it dry. Kaj did the same. By then the coolamon was empty. No water was left for Spinifex.

There was only one thing to be done. They must stay cool and lose as little moisture as possible. The people went to lie down under the shadiest trees they could find. They dug away the warm surface sand near the roots and lay against the cooler sand underneath. Lilil made her baby as comfortable as she could, covering her little body with sand to protect her from the heat. Yinti and Wara lay together under a turtujarti tree that cast a good shade.

'What if there's no water at the next place as well?' said Wara, anxiously.

'There will be,' Yinti assured him. 'Lilil knows. It's a jila, living water, not like this one. Rain or no rain, we'll get a drink.'

After this, the boys lapsed into silence, sometimes dozing, sometimes lying awake trying not to think about their thirst, while the day wore on.

Spinifex found herself a smaller tree nearby and did the same as the human beings. She dug a deep hole by the roots, then lay down inside it and went to sleep.

The sun moved slowly down towards the west, the shadows stretched out further and further, pointing eastwards, and the heat at last began to lose its strength. The people stirred.

'Come on, we'll have to start moving,' said Kaj.

Yinti groaned and sat up. Lilil brushed the sand from her baby, picked her up and fed her from her breast. Her elder daughter started to cry for a drink as well, but she was too big now to take her mother's milk.

'Don't cry,' said Wara, trying to comfort her. 'We're all thirsty, but we'll soon find water.'

'Not today, we won't,' muttered Kaj.

Soon they were all standing and ready to continue their journey. Spinifex got up, stretched and shook herself, and when the people started walking on, she followed.

They all had dry mouths and no one talked much. Yinti picked up a smooth stone and put it in his mouth. Sucking it made his saliva flow and eased his thirst.

They walked through the late afternoon and right through dusk until night fell. The moon, not far from full, had risen early and there was enough light for them to see where they were going. In the cool of the night they picked up speed.

At last the children were too tired to go any further and Lilil's husband decided it was time to stop. Still with no water, the family and Spinifex lay down and tried to sleep. The only person to have a drink was Lilil's baby, who again sucked at her mother's breast.

They were all awake before dawn with parched throats. Without speaking, without thinking about food, they set off again at a steady pace. Spinifex loped along behind, tongue lolling.

By mid-morning clouds were gathering in the north and there were growls of thunder. They watched the sky, but there was no wind and the storm approached with maddening slowness.

'It might miss us,' said Kaj, unwilling to lose time by waiting.

They pushed on. They were not yet within sight of the next living waterhole, but they must be getting close. Spinifex could sense the people's urgency and her own pace quickened. But now the low, dark clouds were covering the sun. There was a rush of cool wind, dust flew, and then the first heavy drops of rain started to fall.

'Water!' said Yinti hoarsely, looking up at the sky and seeing the columns of rain tumble towards him. He and the other children stood with their mouths open, trying to catch the raindrops as they fell. They licked the water that trickled down their arms. Lilil placed her coolamon on the ground and waited. Within moments the slow rain turned into a downpour and soon the coolamon was brimming. Meanwhile, her husband had been at work with his hunting stick, breaking up a pavement antbed that formed part of the ground. He struck it repeatedly, then scraped out the broken pieces, which left a shallow hole. Rainwater drained into the hole and formed a pool. While his wife gave water from her coolamon to the children, Kaj knelt down and drank straight from the pool he had made.

Spinifex didn't wait. She ran around until she found a patch of hard ground where the rainwater formed little rivulets before draining away into the sand, and she lapped the water thirstily. Her tongue became red from the dirt.

By now everyone's body was dripping with water and their hair was soaked. The people shivered with cold.

'Come on, let's shelter!' sang out Lilil.

Leaving the coolamon standing in the rain to catch more water, they ran to take cover in the side of a sandhill, facing away from the storm. Lilil found a spot where the sand had banked up around the roots of a clump of bushes, forming a natural barrier against the wind. Spinifex shook the rainwater from her coat and found her own little shelter against some wattle trees, where she dug herself a shallow cave. People and dog all watched the jagged spears of lightning and braced themselves for the claps of thunder that followed almost at once. After a while, the intervals between the lightning and the thunderclaps grew longer, wind and rain diminished and the storm passed.

From then on, rain fell nearly every day and there was no further shortage of water. Each morning, Spinifex went hunting and brought one or two goannas back to camp. There were plenty of animal tracks near each new waterhole they visited. Clearly, no people had lived in that part of the country for a very long time.

'Good girl, Spinifex!' Lilil said when the old dingo arrived with meat. She then gutted the lizards, singed their skin in the morning fire and cooked them.

Most waterholes were within less than a day's walk of

the next and the people had time to hunt as they went, stopping to cook what they caught on the way. They usually spent one night at each waterhole and moved on the next day. Once or twice, when they had walked further than usual and felt like a rest, they stayed camping in the same place for a few days. From the camp they went into the surrounding countryside to hunt for game and Lilil usually brought back bush fruits as well.

If there was any cooked meat left over at the end of the day, Lilil put it up in the fork of a tree for people to finish off in the morning. Often ants got into it overnight, but it was easy enough to singe them off in the fire. Spinifex hated ants. If she found meat with ants crawling on it, she had to get rid of them before she could eat it. She picked up the meat between her teeth, shook it hard and tossed it into the air, all in one quick movement. When the meat hit the ground, most of the ants were knocked off. Then she grabbed the meat and ran with it before the ants she had knocked off could climb up her legs and attack her. When a stray ant did get into her fur and bite her, she would suddenly jump up and give herself a shake, or swing her head around and bite savagely at the place that hurt, in an effort to kill the ant.

Chapter eight

As the travellers went further north, the country changed. The sandhills became smaller and further apart and the ground flattened out. Eventually there were no more sandhills. The ground was hard and covered with a layer of small pebbles. Ahead they could see long ranges of hills, higher and more massive than any they knew in the sandhill country.

Spinifex was a little uneasy at being so far from the country familiar to her. She came across tracks of animals she didn't know — big animals, to judge by the smell of them and the size of their droppings. These new scents were exciting and disturbing at the same time.

A day or two later, Spinifex saw her first bullock. It was a huge animal, much bigger even than an emu. It stood in one place, staring at her. She approached it cautiously, with flattened ears, ready to bolt if it turned on her. But when the bullock saw the dingo coming close, it turned and started to run away. Then Spinifex knew the animal, for all its bulk, was not dangerous. She went racing after it until Yinti and his sister called her back.

'Leave it!' said Lilil. 'You can't catch a bullock!'

'He might get angry and rip you with his horns,' said Yinti, who had never seen a bullock before either, but had heard about them from his sister and her husband.

'True?' asked Wara. 'Can they really kill you?'

'The bulls are the dangerous ones,' Lilil told him. 'But just keep out of their way and they'll leave you alone.'

The next day they reached a strange place. Spinifex had never come across anything like it before, though clearly it was built by human beings. It was an enclosure made from wooden posts and lengths of wire. Nearby stood a huge structure, taller than any tree, with moving arms that turned in the wind, making a fearful clattering noise. Spinifex flattened her ears when she saw it and crouched down, but the human beings didn't seem afraid.

'Whatever is it?' asked Wara, staring up in amazement at the turning arms.

'It's a windmill,' Kaj told them.

They all followed him right up to the foot of the great structure. Kaj explained how the windmill worked.

'The wind makes the arms go round.' He showed the boys how, as the arms turned, they drove a rod up and down, bringing water up from underground.

They watched the water gushing out from a long pipe into an overflowing trough. It was more water than the two young desert boys had ever seen in one place. Spinifex came up cautiously from behind the human beings, then turned her head sideways and drank straight from the overflow.

The smells around the enclosure were overpowering. Many cattle had been in there recently and there were other strange scents too. Spinifex could detect another large animal, different from the cattle, with rounded hooves. There were also the fresh tracks of two human beings — the first human signs they had come across since leaving Kajamuka. One smelt similar to the people Spinifex knew, but the other smelt quite different. Even his tracks were strange. Spinifex didn't know it yet, but the second man was a kartiya, and he was wearing boots.

All these things were new to Yinti, and his cousin as well. They walked all around the yard, examining the tracks of the cattle and the horses. They inspected the

fences, especially the strands of wire that ran between the wooden posts and rails, holding them together. They stood looking up at the windmill, watching the sails go round whenever the wind blew. They saw all the rungs that ran up the side of the windmill to the top.

'That's a ladder,' Kaj said. 'People can climb up there and fix the windmill if it gets damaged.'

But neither Yinti nor Wara had ever climbed anything taller than a desert tree, and neither was game to try going up the windmill.

So this, at last, was station country. But the travellers still had a long way to go before they would find the main camp where all the station people lived. They followed the tracks of the two station workers and their horse, who could only be half a day ahead of them. Yinti's brother-in-law walked ahead confidently; he had worked on the station and he recognised the barefoot tracks as belonging to a man he knew. But Yinti, Wara and Spinifex went cautiously, troubled by the nearness of strangers.

Later that day, when evening was coming in, the travellers almost caught up with the two men, but they hung back, not wanting to be seen. From the safety of a clump of trees, Yinti and Wara watched the strangers make camp.

'Look at that kartiya,' whispered Yinti, giggling. 'You can see the blood through his skin!'

'Yes, he looks like a ghost,' said Wara.

'Or a gecko,' Yinti said.

The two boys snorted, trying to smother their laughter. They stayed looking at the men as they unsaddled the horse and laid out their blankets and arranged around them all sort of other things whose use or purpose was a mystery to the boys.

After a while, curiosity satisfied for the time being, they backtracked to rejoin the others. They found the family settling down to camp in a sheltered spot on low ground, where their cooking fire would be hidden from sight. Lilil had already cooked the game they'd caught on the trail that day.

When the meal was over, Yinti's brother-in-law got up, saying a few words to his wife. Then he left the others by the fire and went off on his own into the darkness. Spinifex followed him.

Silent as the other animals of the night, man and dog moved fast across the country towards the place where the two station workers were camping. Their fire had burned down to glowing coals and the men had settled themselves for the night. One swag lay on the ground near a tree, while the other was closer to the dying fire. Spinifex could tell from their different scents which man was which.

As Kaj and Spinifex approached the camp, two dogs set up a loud and anxious barking. Spinifex's back prickled and her hair stood up. Her tail dropped between her legs and she slunk back to wait in the safety of the scrub.

Kaj approached the swag near the fire, but his countryman was already awake. Without making a sound, he sprang up. The two men greeted each other silently and moved away from the camp. Spinifex stayed lying in the grass, watching.

The men, almost invisible in the darkness, stood talking in low voices. Then the station man slipped quietly back to his camp while Kaj waited. In a little while, the man was back carrying a bundle, which he handed to Kaj. The two exchanged a few more words, then Kaj turned to go. When he passed close to where Spinifex was lying, the dog jumped up and followed him. She could smell meat and some other, unfamiliar food in the bundle Kaj was carrying.

Back at their own camp, everyone was still awake, sitting around the dying coals of their fire. Kaj showed them what his friend had given him — a lump of cooked bullock meat, some dry damper made from kartiya flour and a package of fine white grains, like sand. Yinti poured some of the grains into a pile in the palm of his hand and licked them up. They were sweet, like honey, and he held out his hand for more.

While the people were eating, they threw scraps of meat and damper to Spinifex. It was the first time she, like Yinti and his cousin, had tasted bullock meat. They all thought it was good.

Next morning, when the two strangers set off again, Lilil's group followed. Both men were now travelling on foot, the light-skinned one leading his horse, and it was easy to keep up with them. That night, they camped near another windmill. After dark, Lilil took her coolamon and went to fetch water from the trough.

Chapter nine

After one more day of following the two men through flat, stony country broken by abrupt hills, the travellers reached the station.

Suddenly Spinifex was surrounded by a bewildering assortment of strange sights and smells. Here were more people than she had ever seen together before, all of them strangers. There was a great deal of noise and confusion. Dogs barked. Spinifex shrank back, ears flattened. She would have run away were it not for the human beings she had come with. They, too, seemed tense, but they kept on going till they were close to the station buildings. They stopped then and waited. Someone had already noticed the little group from the bush and, as the news spread, people came over and stood staring at them. Then a couple of men approached the newcomers. Spinifex hung back, but her companions stood their ground. Kaj greeted some people warmly. They seemed to be friends.

From that moment, everything changed for Spinifex, and for the human beings she had travelled with so far. There was no more hunting. These new people always had food, plenty of fresh bullock meat and damper they made from flour. Instead of separating into ones and twos and walking for long distances every day in search of game, the people all stayed together in one place. They spent a lot of time sitting and talking. Every night they slept in the same camps. Spinifex's human family now wore clothes over their bodies like the other station people and covered themselves with blankets at night. Though the daytime weather was still very hot, sometimes the air grew cold in the early hours of the morning, especially following a rainstorm.

The first chilly night, Spinifex crept onto Yinti's blanket for warmth and curled up behind his knees. Yinti awoke to find her pressing against him, shivering.

'You cold, old girl?' he said, giving her a cuddle. From then on, the dog shared Yinti's blanket every night.

The other dogs that lived at the station did no

hunting. They lay around the camp for most of the day, sleeping and scratching themselves, or wandered around looking for scraps of food. Whenever anyone approached their camp, they set up a loud barking. At meal times, when people threw morsels of food to them, they fought among themselves. Spinifex kept clear of them as much as possible, but now and again a camp dog wandered up to sniff at her. She would curl her lip and pucker her muzzle in warning, then cautiously sniff back. Spinifex was a dingo and didn't bark. She found the station dogs, with their incessant noise, unsettling.

Indeed, station life was altogether too noisy and confusing for Spinifex, who became nervous and edgy. There were so many people — so many children ready to tease the dogs or throw stones at them when they came too close looking for food.

And there were the motorcars. Spinifex never got used to the cars. The first time she ever heard one coming, she ran off to hide in the bush at the edge of the camp and lay watching the noisy monster hurtle along the station track. Even once she got to know them, Spinifex remained wary of the station cars and trucks. She never went near them, even when they were stationary. If one of them came her way, she always ran for cover till it had gone past. She felt ill at ease in this new place, so different from the quiet sandhills she was used to.

Then one day the mail plane flew in. Spinifex heard its roar, like a distant car, long before it reached the station. She pricked her ears and looked troubled. The noise got louder and louder. When the great metal brute circled overhead and then came in to land, plunging down from the sky with a roar louder than thunder, it was too much for Spinifex. With her ears flattened against her head and panic in her heart, she fled from the camp as fast as her feet could take her, away from the pain and terror of that noise, that monstrous flying thing, to the safety of the bush.

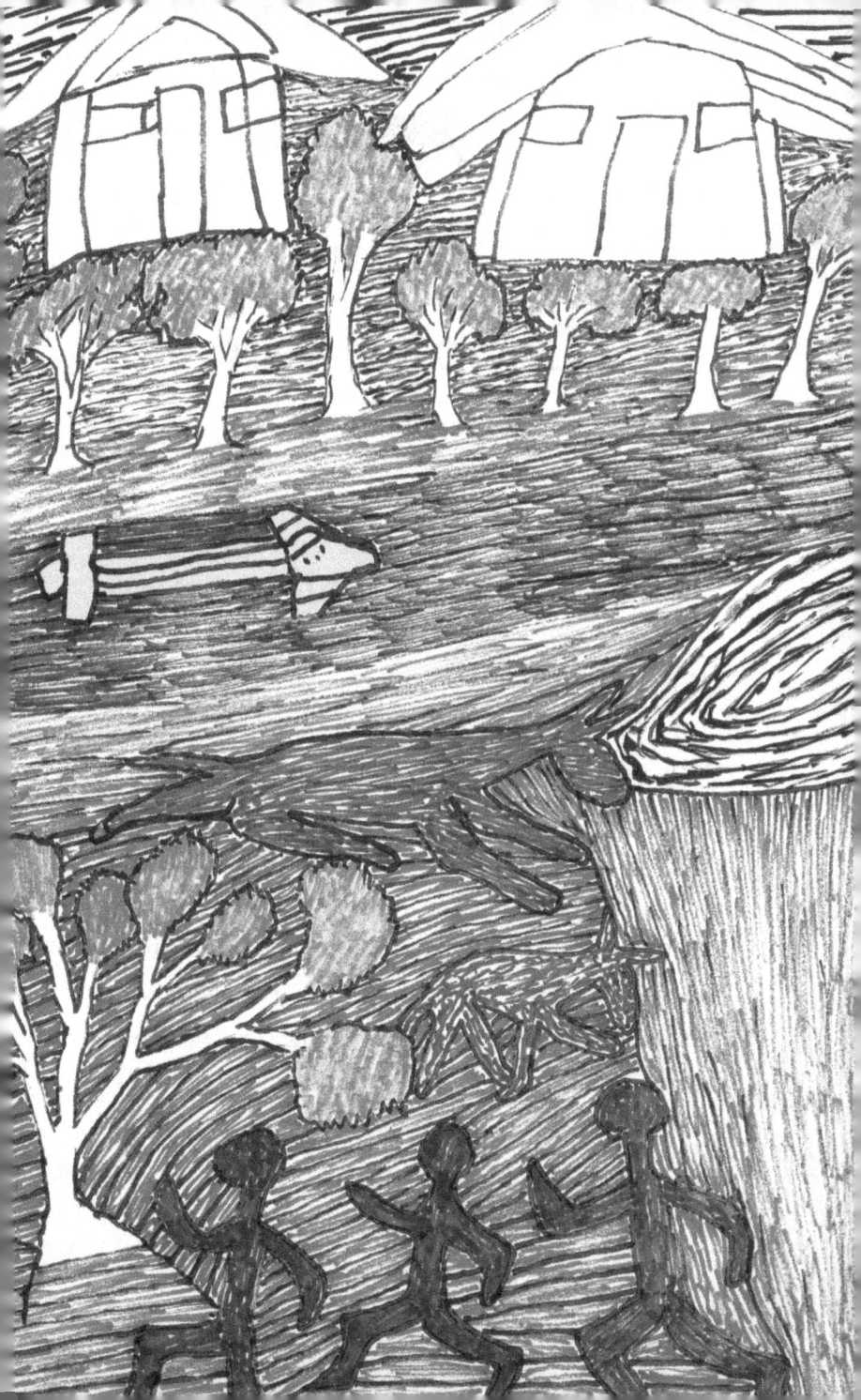

Chapter ten

Yinti saw Spinifex racing away from the camp when the aircraft flew in. He called to her, but nothing would stop her panic-stricken flight.

Later in the day, when the mail plane had long ago taken off again and Spinifex had not returned, Yinti went to look for her. He and Wara walked all around the outskirts of the camp, calling and whistling, but she didn't come. They tried to follow her tracks, but there had been so many dogs and people moving about that her footprints had been covered up. That night, when everything was quiet, they waited for her to come home. But she didn't come.

After a few days, when Spinifex still hadn't turned up, Yinti and his sister gave up hope.

'Those kartiya put down poison for wild dingoes,' one of his uncles told Yinti. 'Maybe your dog got hungry and ate a poisoned bait.'

'Poor old Spinifex,' said Lilil. 'We should have left her with our mother. She didn't like leaving her own country.'

It was holiday time on the station. The kartiya called a stop to most of the station work at this time of year, which had a special name — Christmas. All the working kartiya, the stockmen and the mill hands, went away. Only the manager and his wife, and a couple of helpers, stayed. They paid off the black workers with a supply of flour, tea, sugar and tobacco. Then everyone was free to go wherever they liked. Some people walked to the next station to visit relations who worked there. The journey on foot took several days and people hunted as they went, stopping to sleep near creeks or waterholes. It was almost like old times. A few people stayed on the station, leaving their camp for a day or two now and then to go hunting. They lived partly on the game they caught, partly on fresh or salt beef provided by the station manager.

Lilil and her husband went away to another station, where other relations of Kaj were living.

'We're going to work there next year,' Kaj told the two boys.

'We'll stay here with our uncles and aunties,' said Yinti.

Yinti and his cousin hung around with the station mob throughout the Christmas holidays. At the end of the wet weather, when everyone else came back to work, the two boys decided to leave. They were not yet ready to settle into station life, and they didn't want the kartiya to know they were there and perhaps put them to work. If that happened, they might never get back to their families in the desert.

It was too late in the season to return to the sandhills. The country was by now starting to dry up and they could not be sure of finding water on the way. They would have to stay somewhere close to the station until the next wet season came around.

A day's walk from the station camp lay a range of hills. Yinti's sister had taken the boys there once or twice. She had shown them a great pool of water that never ran dry. A few people who had come in recently from the desert, but who did not want to settle in the station camp, used this rockhole as their base. Many birds and other game were attracted to the stream that flowed from the rockhole, and hunting was good.

Yinti and his cousin moved out to join the other campers at the rockhole, taking with them their blankets and station tools. They made spears from tall, slender trees that grew nearby and again took up the hunting life they had, for a time, left behind. They still visited the relations they had got to know during their weeks at the station. These people made them damper to eat and gave them salt beef to take away with them. But the deep rockhole and the hills around it became the boys' new home.

•⋅⋅•⋅⋅•

The days went by. The moon grew fat and then thin again many times and the seasons changed. The nights became colder and Yinti, lying by his fire wrapped in his blanket, missed the cosy warmth of Spinifex sleeping next to him. The strong easterly winds blew in from the desert and the station country became dry and bare, as the cattle grazed it to dust. No rain fell, but the waterhole in the hills never ran dry.

As the weather once again started to get warmer and the evenings to lengthen, Yinti and Wara became restless for their country. They wanted to go home. Late in the year the air gained moisture and the sky was seldom without a few clouds somewhere on the horizon. The clouds grew denser; the heat increased. Soon the rain would start.

At last, it came: a few violent and squally storms at first, the rainwater quickly sucked up by the thirsty ground. Yinti and his cousin waited. Christmas was approaching again and the station people were preparing for their holiday. Yinti had been away from his country for more than one full year. Now he longed to return, but he couldn't set off until he knew the waterholes had been refilled. He watched the southern horizon each day for rain clouds.

Then came several days of steady, widespread rain and Yinti and Wara knew the time had come to go back to the sandhills. They walked in to the station camp once more to say goodbye to the friends they had made and to tell them their plans. Relations gave them as much beef and damper as they could carry for their journey. At length, the pair set off.

Chapter eleven

The two boys had grown taller since the previous year. After the months they had spent looking after themselves in the hill country, they felt quite confident about the journey ahead. Even so, it would be the first time they had travelled so far without the company of adults. Yinti could picture the surprise on his mother's face when she saw her son, now so much bigger and more experienced than when he had left, arrive back alone with Wara.

'Wait till Kana sees us,' he said to Wara. 'He'll be asking so many questions about the station. He's sure to want to come back with us next time.'

Though they had only travelled that way once, on their journey north the previous year, the two boys had no trouble retracing their steps to the same waterholes they had stopped at then. As before, each morning they set off in the early hours, walked until the sun was high, then rested until later in the day before going on. They hunted as they went.

They were right in their judgement of the amount of rain that had fallen to the south. No waterhole failed them. Travelling on their own, they made good progress. But some days they had to spend a lot of time tracking game.

'We need that old dog to hunt for us,' said Wara. He still wouldn't mention the dingo by name, in case he upset Yinti. 'Remember how she used to bring meat back to camp nearly every morning?'

'True,' said Yinti. 'My mother's going to feel sorry when she hears what happened to her favourite old hunting dog. She'll say we didn't look after her well enough.'

The youths reckoned that their families would again be camping somewhere near Kajamuka. They'd have spent the dry months within reach of a good permanent waterhole and there were only a few of these to choose from in that part of the country. Once the rain started, they would have begun to move out. But, with so few people still living and hunting in the desert, there would be plenty of game and other food and they'd be able to stay for a good while around the same region. Kajamuka was well supplied with trees for shade and firewood and, though only a jumu, its water was deep and lasted long.

As they approached Kajamuka, they found signs to show their reasoning was right. Tracks not more than a few days old could still be seen. Though recent rain had partly obliterated the footprints, the boys could still make out where the sand had been disturbed.

They came to a claypan half-filled with water.

'Look!' said Wara. 'Your mother's tracks!'

Sure enough, in the mud at the edge of the claypan were the familiar imprints of Yinti's mother's feet.

'Poor old Mum,' said Yinti, suddenly longing to see her.

At a nearby camp they found the ashes of fires, not yet covered by blown sand, and bones left from a recent meal. From there, all the cousins had to do was to follow the tracks left by the members of their families. They could tell at a glance which way their relations had gone and, if they needed further proof, ashes from more recent fires at the next camping place soon gave it.

At length, they caught up with tracks only a few hours old and knew they would soon be back with their parents. They walked faster.

Suddenly, Wara pointed.

'Look!' he said.

Smoke was rising from a sandhill not far ahead. Someone was preparing a meal. They were going to arrive just at the right time.

From her camp on the next sandhill, Yinti's mother saw them coming. She watched her son and his cousin, taller than when she had seen them last, and heavier, swinging across the plain below. So, they had come back safely. As they drew closer, she stood up to welcome them, tears spilling from her eyes.

Yinti and Wara walked up the side of the sandhill, grinning broadly. Kana ran forward shouting, and soon the boys were surrounded by their families, everyone talking and asking questions. Then a dog came stepping cautiously towards them, sniffing intently. She was a sandy-coloured dingo bitch. Suddenly, her tail started wagging joyously. Yinti stared at her in disbelief, then bent down and hugged her close. It was Spinifex.

Chapter twelve

When Spinifex fled the mail plane, she ran in panic for a long way, instinctively heading south, towards the desert from which she had come. She didn't stop running until she had left all the noises and smells of the station far behind.

After the strain of recent days, it was a relief for her to find herself back in the open spaces, to hear only the familiar sounds of the birds and the wind. She slowed to a walk, her tongue lolling. Only once did she glance back over her shoulder towards the station. Though she knew her human family was still there, nothing would induce her to go back. The decision was made — she was going home.

It wasn't hard for Spinifex to find the trail she had taken with the people as they travelled north. She was a dingo, with all a wild dog's instincts and independence. Her life amongst human beings had not made her senses and intelligence any less acute. Even so, she had got used to people and in her mind she held an image of the human being who had always meant the most to her — the woman Mala.

Spinifex travelled a lot faster than she had been able to do when she was part of the group with Yinti and his sister, and she made fewer stops. She walked mainly at night and rested during the heat of the day. The only times she deviated from her route was when she had to hunt for meat. She wasted no more time on feeding herself than she had to. She was more intent on finding water each day to quench her thirst. This wasn't hard now that rain had fallen. She just had to find a claypan or one of the waterholes the people had dug out on the journey north.

She headed straight for Kajamuka, the last camp she had shared with Mala. No one was there. Spinifex drank from the waterhole, then sniffed around. The faint scents of people told her they had been there not too long ago and which way they had gone. But she was tired from travelling, the day was getting hot, and she climbed up to a shady tree on the side of a sandhill and flopped down to rest.

When Spinifex woke up, she lay looking out over the desert she knew so well. As far as she could see stretched red sandhills dotted with the spinifex from which she had got her name. Nothing moved. From its hidden perch in a nearby tree, a bird called. The old dingo got up, had another drink from the waterhole and set off again following the trail.

At dusk, the insects struck up their chorus. Spinifex paused and sniffed the air. She could smell a trace of wood smoke drifting from the south. She headed towards it, picking up speed, trotting silently and swiftly through the gathering darkness.

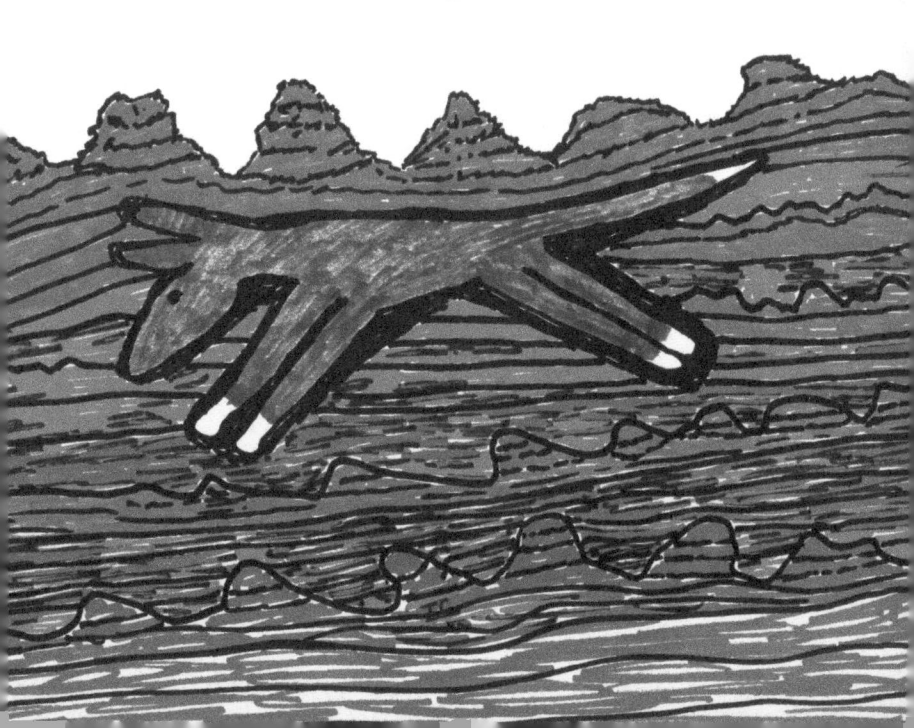

Mala was asleep in her camp when Spinifex found her. She awoke to feel the old dog's muzzle against her neck. She sat up, startled, and Spinifex jumped on her like a puppy, her tail thrashing, and playfully tugged at Mala's arm. Even in the dark, Mala knew the old dog at once.

'Old girl, you've come back!' she said. 'Where's Yinti? Did you bring him with you?' Then she woke her younger son.

'Kana, Kana! Spinifex is here!'

'What?' said Kana, unwilling to let go of sleep.

'My dog has come back!'

'Does that mean Yinti and Wara and the others are here too?'

Kana was puzzled. He knew they weren't intending to come back so soon. What could have happened? He got up and stood staring into the darkness to the north but could see nothing. He called out as loudly as he could, but the only reply came from his uncle in the next camp.

'What's wrong?'

'No, nothing,' Kana called back. 'I thought someone was coming.'

'I think the dog came back on her own,' said Mala. 'Maybe something's happened to those two boys.' She started to weep.

'The kartiya might have killed my son!'

'No,' said Kana. 'Lilil and Kaj will look after him. They know the kartiya. Maybe Spinifex didn't like the station. Maybe she just missed her country.'

As soon as it was light, Kana retraced the dog's tracks for a good way, until he was sure she had been travelling alone.

'She came back on her own, true enough,' he said later to his mother. 'No sign of anyone else.'

'That's what I thought,' said Mala. 'I hope everything's all right. Maybe Yinti will come next year.'

And next year, Yinti came.

A note on Walmajarri words

Walmajarri words carry the stress on the first syllable. We therefore say *Ma*la and *Wa*lmajarri, *Li*lil and *tur*tujarti.

Most of the names used in this book are pronounced more or less as they are written. The name Yinti, however, sounds to English speakers more like Yindi. In Yinti's own language, Walmajarri, there are not two separate t and d sounds, but only one, which falls somewhere in between and is written t.

turtujarti (desert nut tree) is pronounced toor-too-jardi (or doordoojardi). The u in Walmajarri sounds like the u in the English word put, not like the u in but.

kartiya meaning person of European descent, may sound more like gardeeya. As with t and d, the Walmajarri language does not distinguish between k and hard g sounds. The English speaker may sometimes hear the sound one way, sometimes the other.

jila a permanent, 'living' waterhole. The water lies underground and people have to dig, sometimes quite deep, to reach it. The distance from one jila to another might be a journey of two or more days. A jila was especially important during the hot, dry season, when temporary waterholes, such as jumu and jiwari, ran dry. Then family groups had to return to one of these reliable waterholes and stay around there, sometimes for months, until rain returned to refill the others. Jila is pronounced jilla (short i).

Japingka The name of a major jila in Yinti's family's country. Pronounced Jubbing-ga. As with t and d, g and k, Walmajarri does not distinguish between p and b sounds. To the English speaker, the p may sound more like a b.

jiwari A shallow rockhole that holds water for a short time after rain. Pronounced jeewari.

jumu A temporary waterhole or soak. As with a jila, the water is underground, and people have to dig to reach it. However, as the dry season goes on, the water in a jumu dries up.

Kaj The name of Yinti's brother-in-law. Rhymes with judge. A is pronounced like a short u, as in the English word but.

Kajamuka The name of a particular jumu. Every major waterhole, jila or jumu, has its own name, and most have stories associated with them.

Pat and Jimmy

Pat Lowe and Jimmy Pike were born within a year or so of one another at opposite ends of the earth, one in an English city, the other near Japingka, a waterhole in the Great Sandy Desert of Western Australia. Pat spoke English and learnt French at school; Jimmy spoke his father's language, Walmajarri, and also learnt to speak Wangkajunga and several other desert languages.

When Pat and Jimmy were small, Britain and Australia were fighting together in the Second World War. In England there were air raids on the cities, the house next door to Pat's was bombed and food was rationed. In the Great Sandy Desert, people had heard from relations that the kartiya, or white people, were fighting a war, and they often saw aeroplanes flying overhead. Once, Jimmy's mother and sister were frightened when they saw something fall from a plane and explode. Otherwise, the desert people's lives went on undisturbed.

Pat's father was a doctor in the British Army until the war was over, and her mother kept house and bought food in shops. Jimmy's father and two mothers were hunters and gatherers. They caught and killed animals for meat and gathered food from the grasses and trees of the desert. They lived and slept in the open and travelled around the waterholes of their country. The desert was their home.

Jimmy was taught to be a hunter like his parents. He learnt how to track animals and how to find his way over the vast distances of his country without ever getting lost. Most importantly, he learnt the exact position of every waterhole, and how to dig for water. He watched his father making tools from wood and he learnt the names and uses of all the plants, birds and animals in the desert. By the time he reached adolescence, he was able to provide for all his own needs.

While Jimmy was learning the skills of a semi-nomadic hunter, Pat was attending a convent boarding school. She learnt to read and write, to do maths and biology and all the other subjects the nuns taught. She also learnt the names of a few common British birds, animals and plants. Most of her learning came from books, but she also learnt how to find her way around a city, catch buses and trains and use banks and post offices.

Desert people wore only a hair belt and a small loin covering. They had no money, and no use for it. They owned nothing except their tools and weapons, which they carried with them when they travelled. Their only means of transport was their feet. English people always wore clothes and shoes. They also filled their houses with a lot of things they bought from shops. Pat's father owned a car.

When Jimmy was an adolescent, he moved out of the desert with his family to live on a cattle station called Cherrabun. All the desert people eventually left the desert. One reason was curiosity; they wanted to see what life on a cattle station was like. They were especially attracted by the food, the flour and the meat, which seemed so abundant and so easy to get. For the first time in his life, Jimmy saw fences and windmills, then houses and cars. He was given his first clothes. A little later, Jimmy was sent to work as a stockman, riding horses and looking after cattle. He started to learn to speak English.

Pat left school and went on to further education. Her first journey away from her country was to France, where she taught English in a school for a year. Back in England, she worked as a postwoman. While Jimmy was riding horses in the Australian bush, Pat rode a bicycle around town, delivering mail to people's houses. After that, she went to Africa for three years, teaching in a secondary school in Tanzania. Pat later studied psychology in Liverpool, but couldn't settle down again in such a cold and crowded country as England. She made up her mind to migrate to Australia, a continent about which she knew very little except that it was warm and sunny, and the home of black people who threw boomerangs and went 'walkabout'. She paid her fare and arrived on a ship at Fremantle Docks in 1972.

Now Jimmy and Pat were on the same continent and both lived in Western Australia. Jimmy was living in and around Fitzroy Crossing. He has worked for many years

on various cattle stations and tried a number of jobs on farms and building sites. He could drive a car and a tractor. He had been to Pundulmurra College in Port Hedland to learn welding and mechanics. In his spare time he enjoyed carving wood, making hunting sticks and boomerangs and spears, which he sometimes sold to tourists. He still went hunting whenever he had a chance.

Like many of his countrymen, Jimmy sometimes had trouble fitting in with the new way of life, especially in town. He started getting into trouble with the kartiya law. He went to court a number of times and eventually was sent to prison in Broome.

Pat's first job in Western Australia was with Community Welfare, then she worked at Fremantle Prison. In 1979 she asked for a transfer to Broome Prison. This is where the paths of Jimmy Pike and Pat Lowe first crossed. Jimmy was released but later he came back to prison and was sent to Fremantle, where he joined the art classes. His art teachers recognised his talent and helped him develop it.

It wasn't until 1986 that Jimmy and Pat went to live together in Jimmy's camp on the edge of the Great Sandy Desert. Their life was very simple. They did not have a house but they owned a motorcar and did a lot of driving and walking in the desert. Jimmy showed Pat his waterholes and taught her about the bush, and about hunting. By now Jimmy had a growing reputation as an artist. While he painted, Pat sat at her typewriter and wrote down what she was learning about the desert. She took a lot of photographs, and Jimmy did drawings and paintings. The result was their first book, *Jilji*.

Jimmy had many exhibitions of his work, in Australia and overseas. He and Pat travelled to the Philippines, China, Namibia, Italy and England, where Jimmy met Pat's father and other relations. They worked together on several more books. One of their books was adapted into a play.

The pair spent a number of years living mainly in Broome with their dogs, a feral cat and a chook. Jimmy continued to paint and Pat to write. At weekends they often went hunting together and continued to visit the desert when they could. Jimmy died in 2002.